D1206509

Pinky, the Cat Who Liked to Sleep

Pinky, the Cat
Who Liked to Sleep

by Kay Boyle

illustrated by Lilian Obligado

The Crowell-Collier Press, *New York*

Collier-Macmillan Ltd., *London*

Pᴵɴᴋʏ is a silver-gray cat. He likes to sit in the sun and watch birds and mice go by. He likes to watch grasshoppers hop through the grass. He likes to listen to crickets singing under the leaves. He watches and listens for a little while, then he goes to sleep. Sometimes he sleeps on the roof of the house, sometimes on a wall in the sun. He has a friend who is a hoptoad. When it is dark, Pinky and the hop-toad sit in the garden and watch the stars come out.

Pinky lived in the same house with a big brown dog called Hannibal. Pinky always

5

washed Hannibal the way his mother had washed him. He began by washing Hannibal's ears. Then he washed Hannibal's eyes and nose, and then his paws. Sometimes Pinky fell asleep while he was washing Hannibal. When Pinky fell asleep, Hannibal lay very quiet until Pinky woke up again.

One warm September day Pinky got on top of a car in front of the family's house. It was a window cleaner's car. There was a nice soft bed of rags on top of the car. Pinky lay down on the bed of rags in the sun. He covered his eyes with one paw and went to sleep. When the window cleaner had washed the windows in the family's house, he got in his car and drove away. He did not know that Pinky was asleep on top of the car.

When it got dark, everyone asked where Pinky was. Hannibal began to look for Pinky. The little girl and the little boy who owned Pinky looked for him in the backyard. They

called, "Pinky, Pinky." Cats came over the
walls and through the gardens and followed
the little girl and the little boy. A yellow cat,
and two black cats, and a tiger cat, and a
snow-white cat came out of their gardens and
followed them, mee-owing.

"Maybe they want to tell us where Pinky is," the little girl said.

"Maybe Pinky will come home when it gets very dark," said the little boy.

But even when it got very dark, Pinky did not come home. The hoptoad sat alone in the garden and watched the stars come out. Hannibal waited a long time by the front door. Nobody knew that Pinky had been carried away on top of the window cleaner's car.

"Maybe somebody took him because of his silver-gray fur," the little boy said.

"Maybe somebody took him because of his green eyes," said the little girl.

Days and nights went by and Pinky did not come home. So the mother wrote a letter to the newspaper. She said her family had lost a cat with silver-gray fur and green eyes and a very loud purr. She said his name was Pinky and he did not kill birds or mice or hoptoads, and that he liked to sleep in the sun.

8

"If you have seen a silver-gray cat with green eyes, please telephone 8546 Turtle Hill," she wrote.

The first person to telephone was the window cleaner. He said that one afternoon last month a silver-gray cat with green eyes had jumped off the top of his car and run down to the beach. So when the father came home from work, the family and Hannibal got into the car and drove to the window cleaner's house. He lived a long way from the family.

He lived in another town in a house near the beach. It was October now, and a cold wind was blowing the waves. Hannibal ran up and down the beach and barked at the waves.

"Pinky, Pinky!" the family called. Hannibal stopped running. He stopped barking and listened to them calling. He looked up and down the beach.

"September was a long time ago," the little

boy said. He and the little girl were disap-
pointed as they went back to the car.

The next person who telephoned was a lady
who had a food store. She said there was a cat
who came every night to eat at the back door
of the store.

"A little skunk lives under the house next
door," the lady told the mother. "I have fed
the little skunk for a long time. Now I give the
cat ice cream to eat, too. They both eat out of
the same plate. Then they go away together,
and they both purr very loudly."

So when the father came home from work, the family and Hannibal got into the car. It was beginning to be winter now. It was almost dark when the family got to the lady's store. They went to the back door, and they saw two shining eyes.

"Pinky, Pinky!" the father called.

"Pinky, Pinky!" the children called.

The eyes moved away, and Hannibal ran after the eyes. He barked and barked. Then the eyes went under the house next door, and Hannibal followed them.

"Pinky, Pinky!" called the mother. But it was only Hannibal who came. They could not see Hannibal coming, but they could smell him. He smelled so strongly that the children ran away from him. They ran back to the car.

"Those were the skunk's eyes you ran after," the father said to Hannibal. Hannibal was unhappy because he smelled so bad. The father said to him, "We will have to wash you in tomato juice before you can get into the car."

The mother bought a big can of tomato juice from the lady who owned the store. The mother and the children washed Hannibal with the tomato juice. Then they put an old

blanket around him. The father carried Hannibal to the car.

"Pinky will be cold in the winter," the little girl said, and she began to cry. The little boy put his arm around her.

"Pinky has warm fur. He will be all right," the little boy said.

For a week no one telephoned the mother about Pinky. Then the next person to telephone was a lady who had a little boy herself. Her little boy had read the letter in the newspaper. He told his mother to call 8546 Turtle Hill.

"A silver-gray cat with green eyes has been asleep on our garden wall for two days now," she told the mother. "The cat has slept for two nights in my little boy's room. He has a very loud purr."

The lady lived much nearer to the family's house than the window cleaner had, and nearer than the lady who owned the store. She

lived very close to the river, she told the mother. So when the father came home from work, the family got into the car to drive to where the lady lived with her little boy. This time Hannibal did not follow them to the car. He did not want to go with them.

"He is afraid he will meet another skunk," the father said.

The family had to drive on a bridge over the river to get to the lady's house. The lady's little boy opened the front door.

"The cat had silver-gray fur and green eyes and a very loud purr," he said to them. "He did not kill birds or mice. He slept two nights in my room with me. But a little while ago, he ran away down the street. He ran down to the river, and then I didn't see him any more."

So the family walked down to the river to look for Pinky. They watched the cars crossing the bridge over the river, but they did not see Pinky.

"Pinky can't get home unless he crosses the bridge," the little girl said.

"Pinky would be too afraid of the cars to cross the bridge," the little boy said.

"Pinky doesn't know how to swim, so what will he do?" asked the little girl.

The little girl and the little boy wanted to stay there and wait for Pinky to come, but the father said it was too late. The mother took their hands.

"Every time someone telephones, Pinky is a little bit nearer home," she said.

For two weeks no one telephoned about Pinky. And then a man telephoned and said he had a boatyard on the river.

"This morning I crossed the river in my boat," the man said. "When I got to my boatyard on the other side, a gray cat with green eyes jumped out of my boat and ran into the boatyard. He must have been asleep under the seat."

"May we drive over and look for the cat in your boatyard?" said the mother.

"Yes," said the man. "Come and look for him. I read your letter in the paper. Maybe it is your cat."

So when the father came home from work the family got into the car to drive to the boatyard. It was very cold. It was November. This time Hannibal wanted to go with them, but when they got to the boatyard Hannibal would not get out of the car. The children called and called him, but he would not come.

"Are there any skunks here?" the father said to the man who owned the boatyard.

"No, there are no skunks," the man said. But still Hannibal would not come.

It was very dark now. The man turned on the lights in the boatyard, and a cat said, "Mee-ow!" The cat was somewhere under the boats. Then another cat said, "Mee-you, mee-yoy!" And another cat said, "Ow-mee, ow-mee!" A great many cats were talking at the same time under the boats in the boatyard. Hannibal heard them and he jumped out of the car.

"Pinky, Pinky!" the children called. "Come, Pinky!"

Hannibal was barking and barking in the boatyard. First one cat, and then three cats, and then six cats, and more and more cats came running out from under the boats. There were black cats, and yellow cats, and tiger cats, and snow-white cats that came jumping and running and flying through the air, but there was no gray cat among them. Hannibal ran after one cat, and then after another cat, and then after another. But he could not catch them. When the cats had run away, the family and Hannibal got back into the car.

"Hannibal, Hannibal," said the mother, "if you do that to cats, Pinky will be afraid to come home."

The little girl and the little boy were very sad.

"There were almost twenty cats in the boat-yard, but Pinky wasn't there," the little girl said.

"But Pinky got across the river," said the mother. "He took a boat across the river, so he is already a little bit nearer home."

It was winter now. When Christmas Eve came, the children hung up a stocking for Pinky. They hung it next to Hannibal's stocking. In Pinky's stocking there was catnip, and a collar of the same green as his eyes. There was also a soft green blanket for Pinky to sleep on when he came home. The little boy and the little girl and Hannibal were happy with their stockings. But Pinky was not there to enjoy his.

And then on Christmas day a lady with a very old voice telephoned the mother. She said there was a silver-gray cat with green eyes sleeping under her Christmas tree. She said he had "mee-owed" at her door on Christmas Eve and she had let him in. The cat had eaten Christmas dinner with her, she told the mother. She was happy the cat had come because she lived all alone. She said the cat purred loudly after he ate his Christmas dinner. The old lady read the mother's letter in the newspaper a long time ago, and so she had telephoned 8546 Turtle Hill to say the cat was there.

"Come over right away," the old lady said. "I live in the big house on top of Strawberry Hill."

It was beginning to snow when the family got into the car to drive to Strawberry Hill. This time they did not take Hannibal with them.

"Pinky will be afraid if you bark at him the way you barked at the cats in the boatyard," the mother said. Hannibal did not like being left behind.

Strawberry Hill was much nearer to the family's house than the boatyard was, and much much nearer than the house by the river, and much much much nearer than the lady's store, and much much much much nearer than the window cleaner's house. So the family did not have to drive very far. When they got to the house at the top of Strawberry Hill, the old lady opened the door for them. It was snowing very hard.

√"Merry Christmas! Come in, come in!" the old lady said.

"Merry Christmas, Merry Christmas!" the mother and father and the children said.

They went into the room where the Christmas tree was, but the cat was not there. They saw the place under the Christmas tree where the cat had been asleep.

"Where can he be?" said the old lady in surprise.

They looked in every room in the house for

him, and they called, "Pinky, Pinky!" But he did not come. Then they went into the kitchen with the old lady. The back door was a little bit open. Outside they saw the tracks of paws where the cat had walked away through the snow. The children were very happy when

they saw them, and they followed the paw tracks from the back door. It was snowing harder and harder now. "Pinky, Pinky!" the children called. The paw tracks led them under the trees, and across the road, and down Strawberry Hill. But by that time the tracks were covered by the falling snow, and the children could not follow them any more.

"If Hannibal had been here, he would have found Pinky," the little girl said, and she began to cry very softly.

"Pinky is getting nearer and nearer to home every day," the little boy said, and he put his arm around her.

"But he won't be able to find his way through the snow," the little girl said.

When they got back to the old lady's house, the little boy said to his mother and father:

"Pinky has gone down Strawberry Hill. The snow covered up his tracks so we could not follow him."

The family said goodbye to the old lady, and got into the car. They said they would come back and see her again. Even if it was Christmas they were not very happy as they drove home through the snow without Pinky.

Winter was over now, and spring was beginning. The hoptoad came out every night. He sat in the garden and watched the stars alone because Pinky was not there.

"Please write another letter about Pinky to the newspaper," the little boy said to his mother.

So the mother wrote another letter to the newspaper. She said the family had lost a silver-gray cat with green eyes who purred very loudly when he was happy. She said the cat never killed mice, or birds, or hoptoads, and that he liked to sleep in the sun.

27

The next day a man telephoned. He said he was the owner of Turtle Hill Zoo. Turtle Hill Zoo was near the family's house. It was a very small zoo. The little boy and the little girl loved this zoo. The man had read the mother's letter in the newspaper. He said a silver-gray cat with green eyes had slept in the elephant house the night before.

"We have three elephants, and the cat was not afraid of them," the man said. "But the cat was afraid when I went in this morning to feed the elephants. The cat ran into the porcupine's cage and that frightened the por-cupine. The porcupine stuck him full of quills."

"We'll drive over right away," said the mother.

"But the cat isn't here any more," said the owner of the zoo. "He ran out of the porcupine's cage with the quills in him. He jumped over the zoo wall."

"We will drive over and look for him," the mother said.

The father was home that day, so the family and Hannibal got quickly into the car. They drove along the road that led to the zoo. The grass was beginning to turn green.

"I saw three green leaves on a tree," the mother said.

"I saw a yellow flower in the grass," said the little girl.

"I saw a mother robin," the father said.

"I saw a father robin," said the little boy.

And then the mother and the father and the little girl and the little boy and Hannibal saw a gray cat walking beside the road.

"Look," said the father softly. He stopped the car. "There is a gray cat," he said.

"But it doesn't look like Pinky," said the little boy.

"It's much too big and too thin for Pinky," the little girl said.

"I don't think its eyes are green," said the mother. She opened the car door.

Hannibal jumped out right away. He did not bark. He walked up to the big thin cat, and the cat did not run away from him. Hannibal lay down in the grass that was begin-

ning to turn green, and the cat came to him. Hannibal licked the cat's face, and the cat licked Hannibal's ears.

"There are porcupine quills in its back," said the mother.

"It is very dirty, and it cannot stand up very well," said the little girl.

The family got out of the car, and the cat turned its head and looked at them. Then they

saw its eyes were green. When they got close to the cat and Hannibal, they could hear the cat's loud purr.

"It is Pinky," the father said. "It took him seven months, but he was nearly home."

"We must get the quills out of him," said the mother.

And that was what Hannibal was doing. With his strong white teeth he was pulling the quills out of Pinky's back.

"Oh, Pinky, Pinky!" said the little girl.

Pinky was busy washing Hannibal's big brown paw, but he stopped long enough to turn his head and say, "mee-ow!"

70657   jB697p

Boyle, Kay
  Pinky, the cat who liked to sleep.

DATE DUE

MAR 8	AUG 21 '66	FEB 3 '71	NOV 4 '81
MAR 22 '67	NOV 6 '68	MAR 15 70	DEC 9 '81
APR 26 '67		DEC 6 '72	
JUN 7 '68	OCT 1 '68	APR 25 '73	APR 28 '82
JUL 12 '67	NOV 12 '69	May 9 73	APR 20 '83
AUG 2 '67	MAR 25 '70	AUG 15 73	MAY 11 '83
OCT 18 '67	APR 29 '70	FEB 26 '75	DEC 5 '84
OCT 25 '67	MAY 20 70	FEB 7 '79	FEB 19 '86
NOV 8 '67	SEP 30 '70	FEB 28 '79	OCT 0 3 1990
APR 3 '68	Ret 10/7/70	SEP 19 '79	
MAY 8 '68	DEC 23 '78	JAN 1 6 '80	